ni hao, kai-lan

Let's Watch the Ants Dance!

adapted by Tina Gallo
based on the screenplay "Kai-lan and the Ants Dance"
written by Sascha Paladino
illustrated by Jason Fruchter, A&J Studios

Ready-to-Read

Simon Spotlight/Nickelodeon
New York   London   Toronto   Sydney

Based on the TV series *Ni Hao, Kai-lan!*™ as seen on Nick Jr.™

SIMON SPOTLIGHT/NICKELODEON
An imprint of Simon & Schuster Children's Publishing Division
1230 Avenue of the Americas, New York, New York 10020
For information about special discounts for bulk purchases, please contact Simon & Schuster
Special Sales at 1-866-506-1949 or business@simonandschuster.com.
Manufactured in the United States of America 1210 LAK
2 4 6 8 10 9 7 5 3
Library of Congress Cataloging-in-Publication Data
Gallo, Tina.
Let's watch the ants dance! / adapted by Tina Gallo ; based on the screenplay "The Ants Dance"
written by Sascha Paladino. — 1st ed.
p. cm. — (Ready-to-read)
"Based on the TV series Ni Hao, Kai-lan! as seen on Nick Jr."—Copyright p.
ISBN 978-1-4424-1332-0 (alk. paper)
I. Paladino, Sascha. II. Ni Hao Kai-lan (Television program) III. Title.
PZ7.G1382Le 2011
[E]—dc22
2010008182

Hello! I am Kai-lan!

I want to show you
something.

Look! The are doing a
ANTS

dance!

Wow, the **ANTS** are good dancers!

I have an idea. The **ANTS** can put on a show.

All of our friends can come and watch the **ANTS** dance!

Will you watch the **ANTS**

dance too? Super!

But there is a lot to do first.

First each 🐜 needs to
ANT

choose a costume.

One likes the costume with

.

SPARKLES

One  likes the costume with

.

STRIPES

One likes the costume with

.

SWIRLS

Bubu likes the costume with .

POLKA DOTS

Bubu says since **he** likes ,

POLKA DOTS

all of the  will wear .

ANTS POLKA DOTS

Now it's time to  the stage

PAINT

wall.

The 🐜🐜 can  the wall

ANTS   PAINT

✿, ✿, ✿, or ✿.

PURPLE BLUE GREEN   YELLOW

One  likes .

ANT   GREEN

One likes .

ANT   BLUE

One likes .

ANT   PURPLE

Bubu likes  .
YELLOW

He says since **he** likes ,
YELLOW

they will paint the wall .
YELLOW

It is almost time for the show!

Now the  ANTS need to choose

something to wear on their

heads.

One  likes the ⬭.
ANT   ROUND HAT

One likes the .
ANT   DRAGON HAT

One likes the .
ANT   CROWN

Bubu likes the  .
FEATHER HAT

He says since **he** likes the

, they each will wear
FEATHER HAT

a .
FEATHER HAT

It is time for the ANTS to dance.

Oh, no! Bubu is the only ANT
who is ready.

The other ants do not want
to dance!

Do you think the  ANTS are
mad because Bubu made all
of the choices?
I think so too!

The did not want to wear
ANTS

 costumes.
POLKA-DOT

The did not want to paint
ANTS

the wall  .
YELLOW

The did not want to wear
ANTS

the  .
FEATHER HATS

Bubu should not make all of the decisions.

He has to give the  ANTS a choice.

Everyone feels happy when they get a choice!

Bubu tells the  ANTS he is sorry.

The ANTS pick out their own costumes.

Everybody looks great!

The  paint the wall
in different colors.

Wow, look at all of the

pretty colors!

The  ANTS choose

what to wear on their heads.

The  ANTS are so happy!

Everyone feels happy
when they get a choice.

Now all of the  are ready

to dance!

ANTS

It's time to sit down and
watch the
ANTS
do a special dance.

Everyone loves watching the  ANTS dance!

Thank you for watching

the  ANTS dance with me.

You make my ♡ HEART

feel super happy!